FRANKIE'S WISH

ONCE UPON A Dance

ILLUSTRATED BY EMILIA RUMIŃSKA

Dedicated to the forests and their magic.

FRANKIE'S WISH: A WANDER IN THE WONDER (A DANCE-IT-OUT CREATIVE MOVEMENT STORY)

© 2022 ONCE UPON A DANCE
Illustrated by Emilia Rumińska - Emi at Work
Based on a Story by Eva Stone. Inspired by the Price Sculpture Forest on Whidbey Island.
All Royalties Donated.

All rights reserved. No part of this publication may be reproduced, distributed, or transmitted in any form or by any means, without the prior written permission of the publisher, except for brief quotations for review/promotional purposes and other noncommercial uses permitted by copyright law. Teachers are welcome to use the story for class; please give ONCE UPON A DANCE credit.

Join Frankie on a journey of magic and self-discovery. Frankie travels to a mysterious Island to make a special wish. Magical creatures help Frankie find the path to the blue feather. Will Frankie's wish come true? Ballerina Konora joins each page to help readers explore movement and learn dance fundamentals.

LCCN: 2022907909
ISBN 978-1-955555-53-1 (paperback), 978-1-955555-52-4 (ebook), 978-1-955555-54-8 (hardcover)
Juvenile Fiction: Fantasy & Magic (Juvenile Fiction: Performing Arts: Dance; Imagination & Play)
First Edition

All readers agree to release and hold harmless ONCE UPON A DANCE and all related parties from any claims, causes of action, or liability arising from the contents. Use this book at your own risk.

Other ONCE UPON A DANCE Titles:
Joey Finds His Jump!: A Dance-It-Out Creative Movement Story
Petunia Perks Up: A Dance-It-Out Movement and Meditation Story
Dayana, Dax, and the Dancing Dragon: A Dance-It-Out Creative Movement Story
Princess Naomi Helps a Unicorn: A Dance-It-Out Creative Movement Story
The Cat with the Crooked Tail: A Dance-It-Out Creative Movement Story
Brielle's Birthday Ball: A Dance-It-Out Creative Movement Story
Mira Monkey's Magic Mirror Adventure!: A Dance-It-Out Creative Movement Story
Belluna's Big Adventure in the Sky: A Dance-It-Out Creative Movement Story
Sadoni Squirrel: Superhero: A Dance-It-Out Creative Movement Story
Freya, Fynn, and the Fantastic Flute: A Dance-It-Out Creative Movement Story
Danika's Dancing Day: A Dance-It-Out Creative Movement Story
Andi's Valentine Tree: A Dance-It-Out Creative Movement Story
Daryl and the Dancing Dolls: A Dance-It-Out Creative Movement Story
The Grumpy Goat: A Dance-It-Out Creative Movement Story
Dancing Shapes: Ballet and Body Awareness for Young Dancers
More Dancing Shapes: Ballet and Body Awareness for Young Dancers
Nutcracker Dancing Shapes: Shapes and Stories from Konora's Twenty-Five Nutcracker Roles
Dancing Shapes with Attitude: Ballet and Body Awareness for Young Dancers

Hello Fellow Dancer,

My name is Ballerina Konora. I love stories, adventures, and ballet, and I'm glad you're here today!

Will you be my dancing partner and act out the story with me, Frankie, and the creatures of the forest?

I've included ideas of movements that could match the story. You can decide whether to use these instructions, the illustrations, or create your own moves. Be safe, of course, and do what works for you in your space. And feel free to simply settle in and enjoy the pictures sometimes too.

If you enjoy this story, I hope you'll check out some of the other *Dance-It-Out!* or *Dancing Shapes* books.

Konora

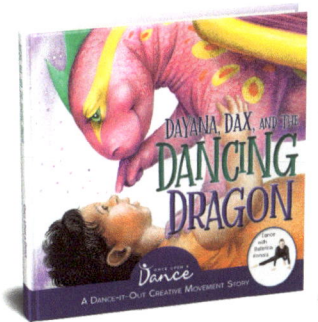
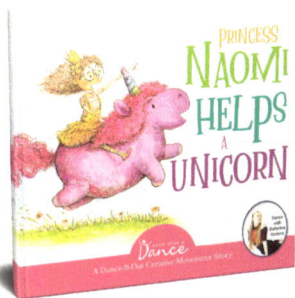
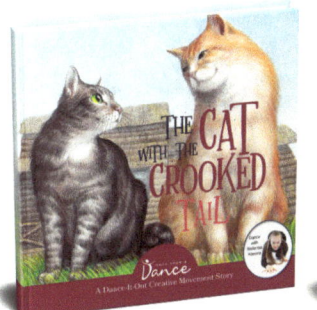
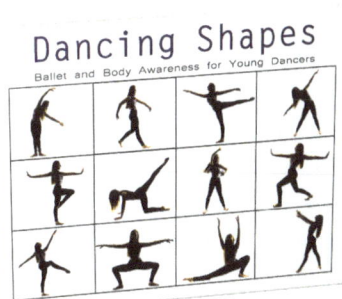

Once Upon a Dance, Frankie lived on Anorac Island in the middle of the sparkling sea. Frankie enjoyed a relaxing island life with Auntie Duke but sometimes longed for adventure.

People told tales of a magic feather hidden on the island to the east. The stories claimed the feather would grant one birthday wish to anyone who found it. Today was Frankie's special day, and Frankie's wish was to be a famous dancer.

Let's act out the story together.

Can you imagine you are the entire ocean, vast and shimmering? The sea can be wild and wavy or calm and still. Which one suits your mood today? Can you create an ocean with your arms, your legs, your head, or your whole body?

It's Frankie's birthday. I'm going to wear my birthday crown and blow out my pretend candles. Can you think of a different way to show a birthday celebration using your body?

Auntie Duke was finishing up in the kitchen as Frankie bounded down the stairs. She'd wished on the feather when she was Frankie's age. "Good luck today. Can I share a little advice?" she said. When Frankie nodded, Auntie continued, "First, use your mind, body, and imagination as you wander in the wonder. Second, ask for help along the way. And third, keep an open mind. Things are not always as they seem."

We can count along with Auntie Duke's advice: one, two, three. Let's touch our forehead to symbolize the mind, move our hands along our bodies, and feel our imagination all around us. Here's my pose for *asking for help*, do you have another idea?

After a quick breakfast, Auntie handed Frankie a backpack. "I packed you a few supplies. I'm looking forward to celebrating your birthday tonight." After a quick cuddle, Frankie headed out. Feeling a little nervous about taking the ferry and going on the birthday quest alone, Frankie stopped to summon courage by shouting to the sky, "I am calm, confident, and capable!"

I am calm, confident, and capable was one of Auntie's mottos. She smiled and nodded from the window as Frankie set off on the birthday adventure.

Give a real or pretend hug, then let your head fall back and reach your chest up to the clouds. Put your hands on your hips and shout "I am calm, confident, and capable!" Hey! That feels great. Maybe I'll say that to myself tomorrow, too.

During the ferry ride, Frankie felt around inside the backpack and found a water bottle, a peanut-butter-and-jelly sandwich, a pencil, notebook, compass, sweater, and best of all, Auntie Duke's homemade caramels.

As soon as the boat docked, Frankie headed toward the arched sign marking the path into the forest. It read *Wander in the Wonder*.

Unzip your backpack and dig around to see what's inside.

To make the arch, which is called bridge pose, we need to practice a few things first. Lie on your back, pull your feet closer in, and bend your knees. Touch your hands to the floor above your shoulder with your fingers pointed toward your body. First, lift only your bottom in the air. Come down and rest. Then lift your chin to your chest and push both your bottom and your shoulders in the air. Once you've practiced that, keep your chin lifted and push your belly higher.

Frankie stopped and read the words out loud, letting them float in the air. Auntie Duke's advice—*use your mind*—echoed in Frankie's head. Maybe *Wander in the Wonder* was a clue? Frankie took out the notebook and wrote the words.

The wind was swooshing through the trees. Frankie reached up to feel the wind's push and pull. *Use your body and your imagination*, Auntie Duke had said. Frankie swayed in the wind, imagining birds soaring above the trees.

Pretend to open and write in your notebook. Reach up and wiggle your fingers. Then imagine a water wave pushing your shoulders sideways in each direction. Turn that sway into a bird soaring with wings opened wide on the wind.

Frankie heard a rustle in the leaves high above and looked up. A silver eagle with outstretched wings was perched on a thin branch. Auntie's voice rang in Frankie's mind: *Ask for help.*

"Hello, I'm searching for the magic blue feather to make my birthday wish. Is this the right way?"

The eagle stared for a long moment, and then replied,

> "The only way to reach your quest is to find the flowers in the west. Enjoy your meal and have some fun. A clue will appear under the sun."

And with a final eagle-eyed stare at Frankie, the bird flapped away. Frankie checked the compass.

Bend your knees and lower yourself, keeping only your feet touching the ground. How low can you go? Reaching your arms out like wings might help you balance. Flap those powerful wings to fly away.

Hold your compass in your palm, pretend to flip open the top, and lean closer to check your direction.

What a magical place! Frankie thought, continuing west along the path. The trail fell and twisted deeper into the forest. The birds chirped, and the sun peeked through branches like golden threads of light. Frankie felt the forest's energy, the busy creatures, and the crisp, fresh air. Overwhelmed with happiness, Frankie twirled in delight.

Toss your arms up and joyfully spin around.

Frankie headed west for nearly an hour. Up ahead, colorful flowers waved their petals in the breeze. It seemed like the perfect place for a picnic.

Frankie found a spot in the shade and took out a sandwich and bottle of water. The flavors frolicked on Frankie's tongue, and the gulps of cool water tasted very refreshing. Sunlight shone through the petals casting red, yellow, and pink on the ground. Suddenly, purple writing appeared!

> The magic feather isn't here. Find a friend you mustn't fear.
> Now turn back and don't be slow. Your friend will tell you where to go.

Frankie packed up the picnic things and headed back toward the forest's entrance. Frankie hoped that turning around wasn't a mistake.

Challenge yourself to sit down without using your hands. Pretend to rummage in the backpack and unwrap and eat your sandwich. Unscrew the water bottle cap to open it, and then tip the bottle to take a drink.

Frankie had only taken a few steps when a sudden, deep rumbling came from the forest floor. The rumbling grew louder and louder. Frankie looked up and gasped in surprise!

A giant T-Rex blocked the path! Its eyes were wide and its open mouth showed sharp, jagged teeth and a vibrant red tongue.

"WHAT ARE YOU DOING IN MY FOREST?" bellowed the T-Rex. "WHO SENT YOU? WHAT DO YOU WANT?"

Imagine you're a heavy dinosaur stomping your strong legs. Don't feel like you have to match me or the pictures as you tell the story. Maybe your dinosaur moves on its knees or on all four limbs.

Frankie was nervous but stood tall and took a deep breath.

"My name is Frankie, and I'm looking for the magic blue feather. Today is my birthday, and I want to make a wish just like my auntie."

The dinosaur looked at Frankie with one gigantic eye then turned its head to look with the other.

There were three paths behind the T-Rex. Gathering courage, Frankie asked, "Do you know which path I should take? Can you help me, please?"

The T-Rex made a loud snorting sound and said, "I will help you IF you can answer my question."

Take a breath in. See if you can pull air down to your toes.

Lean closer and turn your head as if you can only see from one eye. Then swoosh your head down and to the other side. Take a quick and noisy sniff.

The T-Rex smiled a toothy grin.

"If a magic wish you hope to find, how should you travel with a curious mind?"

Frankie stood puzzled. Without an answer, would the adventure end in failure?

"Chewing helps me think," said Frankie, reaching into the pack and pulling out two caramels. Frankie offered one to the dinosaur who politely shook its head and said, "No, thank you."

Frankie unwrapped and chewed a caramel.

Unzip your backpack and reach to the bottom to find two treats. Hold one out to your new friend, then unwrap it, pop it in your mouth, and chew. Let's move like a caramel, slow and ooey-gooey. Try twisting around by reaching a part of your body in a new direction.

Like a lightbulb switching on, the answer came.

"You must wander in the wonder!" Frankie said with a laugh.

The T-Rex stood up and flapped its tiny arms with joy. "Well done! Here's your clue," it said with another toothy grin.

"Take the path you know is right. You'll find a friend who's just your height. They'll help you cross a place that's wide. Follow their lead to the other side."

Then, with a flourish of its tail, the T-Rex disappeared into the trees.

Keep your elbows attached to your sides and flap your hands up and down in front of your body like the T-Rex.

"But wait! I don't know which path is right!" Frankie called out. But the dinosaur was gone.

Frankie looked at the three paths, shrugged, and let out a sad sigh.

But after writing the words in the notebook, Frankie smiled at the dinosaur's play on words. "Very clever. The right path is the RIGHT path." Auntie Duke had shown Frankie how to stretch a thumb and pointer finger out on each hand. The hand that looked like the letter L was the left one. Frankie took the opposite path.

Lift your shoulders toward your ears and put your hands out to the side.

Sigh through your nose and give a little laugh. Put your hands up and close together, then reach your pointer finger and thumb out like the letter L and its mirror image.

It wasn't long before the path came to a sudden end at the edge of a wide, tree-lined canyon. Vines hung overhead, and Frankie was tempted to swing across. But would the vines be strong enough?

Frankie turned around to look for clues and noticed a figure perched on a tree stump. It was hard to make out in the shadows, but it looked like a gorilla. Remembering Auntie Duke's advice to keep an open mind, Frankie asked, "Hello, is someone there? Can you please help me?"

Squat down, then sway like a heavy gorilla—move your foot sideways with each step forward. It's tricky to move in your low shape with your knees bent. Touching the ground helps.

"I'm Gorilla Joe," said a silver beast as he ambled closer. The gorilla was as tall as Frankie, but seemed much bigger. Gorilla Joe grabbed a vine with his big left hand and swung to the next. From left and right, he swayed across the canyon, singing in a deep voice that echoed around the jungle.

"Swing with me and here's my clue. Left, then right is what you do. Don't be scared, just follow my lead. On the other side is what you need."

After watching which branches the gorilla grabbed, Frankie followed the same path, swinging from vine to vine, until they were both safely across the valley. Frankie thanked the gorilla and waved as he vanished into the woods.

Reach up, and use your right hand to grab a vine. Then grab another with your left as you take a step like you're swinging across a jungle. When you reach the other side, wave goodbye to your new friend.

As Frankie wrote in the notebook, the wind picked up and the sun lowered in the sky. Frankie raced down the path, hoping to get home before dark. *The magic blue feather must be near.*

Turning a corner, Frankie saw golden light shining over a clearing. Frankie ran to the sunlit patch and read the nearby sign: *Dance Your Journey.*

The words in the notebook were clear in Frankie's mind. *I think I should dance my day from the beginning.* Frankie put the pack down and formed an arch like the one near the forest entrance.

Next, Frankie stretched both arms and swayed in the breeze, flapped like the giant eagle, danced like the flowers' shadows, and jumped into a powerful stance like the T-Rex. Frankie swung like Gorilla Joe, then let loose in a swinging, swirling, twirling, jumping, joyful celebration.

Can you remember some of the moves we practiced together? Start with the bridge pose and be sure to tuck your chin. Once you've danced like the magical creatures, make up your own dance. Add some spins and jumps for extra fun.

Frankie was so lost in the dance that it took a moment to realize the sun had shifted and the golden light had vanished. Frankie whispered to the forest, "Thank you for the inspiration. It made my dance special. I'm grateful for all I have and all I have learned."

Though it wasn't dark, the sun had settled deep behind the trees. A beautiful blue light peeked through the branches. Frankie picked up the backpack and set off toward the glow.

Take a moment to feel gratitude and appreciate your body, your home, and your family.

After only a few more steps, there it was...the magic blue feather sparkling on the forest floor. It was unusually large, as if it came from a giant mythical creature.

The gorgeous blue light gave off a slight warmth, and Frankie basked in its glow. The moment for the birthday wish had finally arrived. Frankie thought about the wonderful day and let out a tired, but happy, sigh.

"Oh, blue feather, I've changed my mind. I wanted to be a famous dancer, but I don't want that anymore. I want to wander my own dance path and find my own inspiration. My birthday wish is to *go home*, so I can tell my auntie about my amazing day."

Reach your hands out like you're feeling the warmth of something in front of you. Breathe in and then let out an extra long breath. Squeeze all the air in your lungs out.

Auntie Duke blinked in surprise. "Whoa! Did you come through the front door?"

"No," said Frankie, looking around. "The magic feather brought me home."

Auntie Duke smiled. "Did you wish to be a famous dancer?"

"No. I realized that making friends, seeing beauty, and solving puzzles were the best parts of my journey. If I become a famous dancer without making any effort, it won't feel as special. Does that make sense, Auntie?"

She nodded and hugged Frankie. "Of course it does. So, what did you wish for?"

"To be here with you," said Frankie, relaxing into Auntie Duke's arms.

"My dear, sweet Frankie," said Auntie Duke. "I am SO proud of you. You are strong, brave, and wise. And I love you with all my heart."

Imagine you've been transported somewhere by magic. Look around at your new surroundings. Cuddle up next to someone for a hug if you like. Or close your eyes, hug yourself, and thank your body and brain for all they can do.

Thee end.
The end.

(My grandpa always ended stories this way and I like to share the fun.)

Thanks for being my dance partner.
Until our next adventure.

Love,

Konora

 P.S. Our wish is for a kind, honest review.

CPSIA information can be obtained
at www.ICGtesting.com
Printed in the USA
BVHW022149130822
644538BV00001B/2